Coral Reefs

by Nadia Higgins

MW00998430

Bullfrog Books

Ideas for Parents and Teachers

Bullfrog Books let children practice reading informational text at the earliest reading levels. Repetition, familiar words, and photo labels support early readers.

Before Reading

- Discuss the cover photo. What does it tell them?

- Look at the picture glossary together. Read and discuss the words.

Read the Book

- "Walk" through the book and look at the photos. Let the child ask questions. Point out the photo labels.

- Read the book to the child, or have him or her read independently.

After Reading

- Prompt the child to think more. Ask: Have you ever visited a coral reef? Have you seen videos or pictures? How would you describe it?

Bullfrog Books are published by Jump!
5357 Penn Avenue South
Minneapolis, MN 55419
www.jumplibrary.com

Library of Congress Cataloging-in-Publication Data

Names: Higgins, Nadia, author.
Title: Coral reefs / by Nadia Higgins.
Description: Minneapolis, MN: Jump!, Inc., [2017]
Series: Ecosystems
Audience: Ages 5–8. | Audience: K to grade 3.
Includes bibliographical references and index.
Identifiers: LCCN 2016056357 (print)
LCCN 2016057726 (ebook)
ISBN 9781620316764 (hardcover: alk. paper)
ISBN 9781620317297 (pbk.)
ISBN 9781624965531 (paperback)
Subjects: LCSH: Coral reef ecology—Juvenile literature.
Coral reefs and islands—Juvenile literature.
Classification: LCC QH541.5.C7 H54 2017 (print)
LCC QH541.5.C7 (ebook) | DDC 577.7/89—dc23
LC record available at https://lccn.loc.gov/2016056357

Editor: Jenny Fretland VanVoorst
Book Designer: Molly Ballanger
Photo Researcher: Molly Ballanger

Photo Credits: Alamy: Carlos Villoch/MagicSea.com, 20–21. Biosphoto: Jean-Michel Mille, 14–15; Mathieu Foulquié, 15. Getty: Douglas Klug, 4. iStock: mihtiander, 6–7. Shutterstock: unterwegs, 1; Nantawat Chotsuwan, 3; think4photop, 5; sergemi, 10–11; ReereeKhaosan, 12; olias32, 12; Rich Carey, 13; frantisekhojdysz, 16; Greg Amptman, 17; Michael Bogner, 18–19; GaudiLab, 23br; aarows, 24. SuperStock: NHPA/Photoshot, 8–9. Thinkstock: jon841, cover.

Printed in China.

Table of Contents

Many Colors

A world of colors hides under the sea.

Where?

On a coral reef!

Coral are tiny animals.
They live near the shore.

reef

shore

coral
shell

Their shells
make the reef.

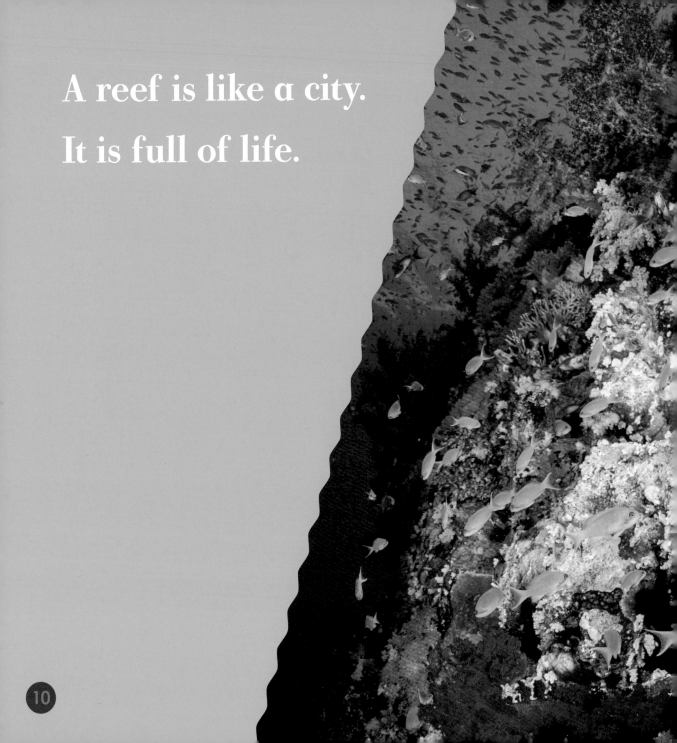

A reef is like a city.

It is full of life.

Many plants live here.

Many animals do, too.

13

Reef creatures help
each other. How?

Algae grow
on the coral.

They give it color.

They make it strong.

algae

Look out, fish!

Here comes a shark!

The fish swim in a group.
It is hard to spot just one.
Together they are safe.

Fish nibble on
a shark's skin.

The fish get a meal.

The shark gets clean.

A coral reef is a world of colors.

It is a world of life.

Dive in!

Where Are the Coral Reefs?

Australia's Great Barrier Reef is the largest coral reef in the world. More than 1,500 kinds of fish live there.

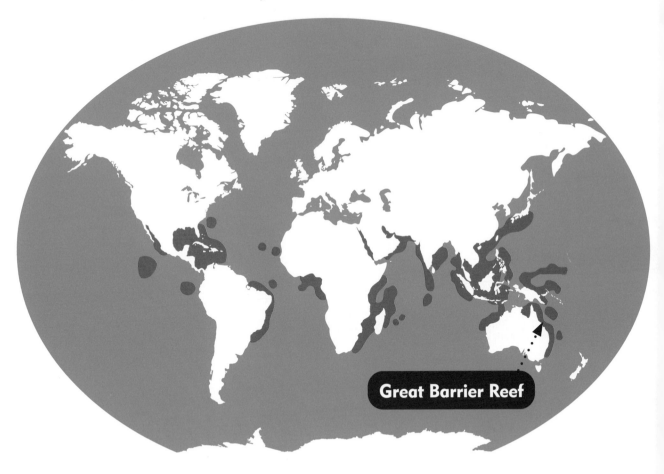

Great Barrier Reef

■ coral reef

Picture Glossary

algae
Tiny creatures that grow on coral; algae need sun to grow, like plants.

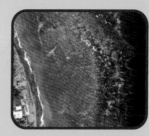

reef
A strip of sand, rocks, or coral that rises near the top of the sea.

nibble
Eat by taking tiny bites.

shore
The place where a body of water meets land.

Index

To Learn More

Learning more is as easy as 1, 2, 3.

1) Go to www.factsurfer.com

2) Enter "coralreefs" into the search box.

3) Click the "Surf" button to see a list of websites.

With factsurfer.com, finding more information is just a click away.